Praise for
Apples of Gold

"Lisa brilliantly weaves the important message of purity into this powerful little parable—a must-read for every young woman you care about!"

—SHANNON ETHRIDGE, MA, best-selling author of *Every Young Woman's Battle*

"Lisa Samson's *Apples of Gold* is the perfect apple of a story—a beautiful tale on the outside with delicious substance underneath! In an age when too many girls are confused about what real love involves, mothers and daughters should not miss this important parable."

—ANGELA HUNT, author of *Uncharted*

"A beautiful tale, simply told, *Apples of Gold* shines with truth. Give this book as a gift to the young girls in your family. You'll be glad you did."

—ROBIN LEE HATCHER, author
of *A Carol for Christmas*

"My fifteen-year-old daughter stayed up late to finish *Apples of Gold*. She loved the story's fairy-tale format, and the message came through beautifully yet subtly."

—DEBORAH RANEY, author
of *A Vow to Cherish*
and *Remember to Forget*

Apples of Gold

A Parable of Purity

Lisa Samson

WATERBROOK
PRESS

APPLES OF GOLD
PUBLISHED BY WATERBROOK PRESS
12265 Oracle Boulevard, Suite 200
Colorado Springs, Colorado 80921
A division of Random House Inc.

The characters and events in this book are fictional, and any resemblance to actual persons or events is coincidental.

ISBN 1-4000-7093-7

Library of Congress Cataloging-in-Publication Data

Samson, Lisa, 1964–
    Apples of gold : a parable of purity / Lisa Samson. — 1st ed.
        p. cm.
    ISBN 1-4000-7093-7
  1. Sexual abstinence—Fiction. 2. Sisters—Fiction. I. Title.
    PS3569.A46673A79 2006
    813'.54—dc22

                                        2006010243

Printed in the United States of America
2006—First Edition

10 9 8 7 6 5 4 3 2 1

With love and prayers
for Ty, Jake, and Gwynnie;
in thankfulness for Joy and
Bill, who chose the better path;
and for Will, who stood strong.

*O*nce upon a time, many years ago, true love walked hand in hand with kisses and promises, and decisions were made to last forever. In such a time, two girls received a summons to appear before the governor. Governor St. Juste tended the island with the gentle care of a loving father. He knew each inhabitant by name, and on the morn of each one's birth, she

1

expected to discover a basket of chocolate and fruit on her doorstep. No one was ever disappointed.

"Are you nervous?" Kate asked her sister as they stood in the governor's palatial waiting room.

"Terrified!" whispered Liza, reaching out for the comfort of Kate's hand.

"But he's always been so kind."

"It's true. Which leads me to wonder what we've done that he should call us before him!"

Governor St. Juste welcomed the young women into his office, a large room paneled in walnut carved with designs of fruit and flowing ribbons. Towering mirrors opposite a wall of windows reflected the blue of the afternoon sky. The appointments of the room appeared almost as magnificent as the governor, but in truth, upon close inspection, the most majestic wood and mirrors could not eclipse the character of the man himself. Even the shining golden medallion of his

office, hanging from a satin band around his neck, did not out-shine the regal air with which he moved or the kindliness that glowed in his eyes.

He beckoned them in with a sweep of his arm. "Liza and Kate, come sit here by my desk. I have something to give you."

The girls, pink with relief and delight, settled themselves upon two chairs facing the gleam-ing surface. They adjusted their skirts just so and crossed their feet at the ankles as their mother

had taught them. They dared not speak, but nodded as though his words held almost as much importance as, "Let there be..."

He eased back in his chair and clasped his hands across the front of his light blue, quilted waistcoat, idly fingering the medallion. "You're both getting older now, you know. Many years ago your father and mother approached me and asked me to set you aside for a special purpose. The time has come for me to fulfill that promise."

Kate, just seventeen, wiggled in her seat and raised her eyebrows at Liza, soon to turn eighteen.

Liza refolded her hands in her lap. "Thank you, sir."

He cleared his throat. "You know your father and I go back to our boyhoods together, don't you? My father's carpenter was his father."

"Yes, Your Grace," Liza said. Father told them often how their family had served the St. Justes for generations. How Father had even saved the governor's

life years ago, before they came of age. Father said a strong bond like no other knit them together that day.

"Yes, well. In a week's time, my eldest son is returning home from his tour of duty with the Royal Navy. He will need someone to care for his house. You're from a good, hearty family, hard workers all. Your parents are responsible, faithful citizens of the island, completely reliable and dependable." He rapped his knuckles on the beautiful desk

the girls' father, a carpenter like
his father before him, had made
only the previous year. "Not to
mention the history between
your father and me. No doubt he's
regaled you with stories of how
much we loved to fish together
and wander the hills."

The girls nodded. If James Carpenter, their father, carried one
regret, it was his inability to step
into the life of his good friend.
Privilege like that belonged to
only a few. On the other hand,
James was known and respected

as a gifted craftsman, which was a privilege in itself.

"All in all, you seem to be strong, able girls."

"Thank you, sir," said Kate.

Her voice echoes sweetly, Liza thought.

"Of course, m'lord," said Liza. Not nearly as pretty as her sister, or as silver throated, she tried to sound as agreeable as she felt. Truly she couldn't remember ever being this excited, this honored. Or this nervous.

"Good, then!" The governor

reached down and opened a desk drawer. From its recesses he pulled out two large wine red apples. Beautiful, shining, perfect specimens of fruit.

Liza had never seen such pleasing food in all her life, for her father, royal carpenter though he was, possessed not the riches for such luxuries. The crimson skin glowed as if from within, and Liza just knew the flesh was the sweetest found anywhere.

"Oh my!" Liza said. "How beautiful!"

The governor nodded. "Yes, quite. Lovely, aren't they?"

Kate reached out. "I'm sure it is the tastiest fruit on the island. I cannot wait to try one!"

The governor's brows leaped toward his hairline. "Oh, but they're not for you. They're for Claude, my son. I'm entrusting them to your care until he arrives, after which time, you'll join him at his home. But we have need for only one of you to accompany my son. It will be up

13

to him to decide between the two of you."

Liza's heart stuttered. To work in the home of the governor's son! More than a simple girl dared to hope for. Only the most trusted citizens of the island cared for those in the governor's household.

Kate thrust out her hands. "Oh, I'll take perfect care of them, Your Grace!"

"Wonderful! But do take only one." And he placed a single apple in her hands. "And what of you,

14

Liza? Will you care for the fruit until his arrival?"

"I'd be honored, sir. But might you hold on to the fruit for just a few minutes more? I shall return with a basket and a length of cloth in which to cradle the apple."

"Good! Good! I like the way you think, Liza."

"Thank you, sir."

Kate immediately held out her apple for the governor to retrieve. "Perhaps this would be safer in Liza's basket as well."

15

"Oh no. No, no. Liza can't take care of your fruit, Kate. That is impossible."

Kate blew out air softly over her bottom lip. "It's such a long walk back to the cottage. I do believe I can hold it tenderly enough on my own."

"As you wish, child. You are the guardian. I will not make you care for it in any other way than how you see fit."

When the girls walked away from his office, Kate displayed the apple with pride and a bit of

bravado. "I'm certain everybody we pass thinks I am the luckiest girl in the world!"

The prettiest, too, thought Liza, as she walked along empty handed. *If not a bit of a show-off.* Certainly Liza appeared out of favor somehow, the girl with neither the apple nor the pretty face. No matter. When Mother and Father needed something done right, they came to Liza. When the children chose participants in schoolyard games, they always snatched up Liza in the first

round, knowing her heart was strong, her aim true. She rarely received invitations to the parties, and never inherited the cast-off clothing of the rich girls the way Kate did, but Liza relished one thought: she was smarter than Kate and knew that prettifying oneself or laughing like a crystal brook didn't ultimately please anyone for very long.

Oh, but Kate could be such fun! And to her credit, she walked slowly enough, even if she was only doing it to show off.

They strolled past the governor's palace and soon came to the smaller house, large by the standards of regular folk, that the governor had commissioned for his son. The girls' father had worked hard on the new interior, and before the final painting was hung in place and the new furniture arranged, he'd guided them on a tour through dozens of rooms. Besides the palace of the governor himself, no finer place existed on the island, Liza was certain.

"I can hardly imagine working here," she breathed.

"I can all too easily imagine it," Kate laughed, "which defines my lot in life! Too expensive a taste for the circumstances."

Liza rubbed her sister's arm. "No doubt someday a rich merchant will come into town, see you down at market, Kate, and fall quickly and completely in love with you."

"I'd rather have the governor's son!" she giggled.

With a final glance at the

house, Liza hurried on ahead to fetch the basket and the cloth from home as quickly as possible. It wouldn't do to keep the governor waiting. Though nice enough, he remained the governor, and who knew what milled inside the heads of powerful men like him?

She breezed into the house where her mother busied herself at the table. "Good afternoon, Mother."

Mother was a comfy woman, with ankles that matched her large heart and eyes greener

21

than the water of the bay. She set down a freshly peeled carrot. "Liza, dear! How did you fare with the governor?"

"Splendidly!" Liza kissed her mother's cheek. "The governor gave us gorgeous apples to tend for his son, who's coming home in a week's time. We may be hired to work in his house!"

"Lovely! It seems like only yesterday Master Claude went away for his stint in the navy. So where is this splendid apple, then?"

Liza related her plan.

"Good thinking, lovey!"

Her father, sanding a freshly built table out in the sun, said through the window, "That's using your noggin! I suppose your sister's still on the way home? Carrying her apple in hand, no less?"

Liza and her mother laughed. But not too long or too hard, for Liza quickly gathered her basket and cloth, then sped out the sunlit doorway back toward the palace.

She passed Kate, talking to Ian, their neighbor.

"Kate! What are you doing?"

Ian held the apple in his hands. True, Liza would never describe him as reckless, but for Kate to take such a chance!

Kate retrieved the apple and tossed her hair. "Ian only wanted to see it. Look! It's just the same."

But Liza noticed that finger-prints, like yeast on a grape, now dusted the shining crimson. "No matter, Kate. You can polish it up

just fine at home. I'm off to fetch mine. Wish me luck."

The two offered good wishes and, smiling, waved her off.

Liza picked up her pace. Hurried past the shops and church. Called only brief greetings to friends and neighbors.

Finally, she waited again outside the governor's office to be summoned inside. When she stood before his desk once more, he nodded and held up a finger. "I have a good feeling about you, Liza. You seem like a young

woman with her head firmly attached to her shoulders. No fooling you, eh?"

"I hope not, Your Grace. I try to keep my wits about me at all times."

"That's plain to see. Well then, here you are. Come get the apple."

"If you would, sir, I have just the spot." Liza stepped forward and opened the lid of her basket. A nest of fabric readied a perfect resting place for the fruit.

"Indeed!" The governor placed the apple just as Liza herself

would have. "Do you know much about my son, Claude?"

"Only that he's been away and that he's favored in your eyes. Father speaks well of him."

"Then you have heard correctly. It's an honor for you to be considered for this position." He laid a hand on her arm. "I have a feeling you'll present him this apple in as fine a condition as you've received it yourself."

"By the grace of God, m'lord."

"Oh, surely you speak the truth. Now, off with you. In one

week's time, on the stroke of noon, Claude will be arriving for the first time at the house built for him. I expect you and your sister to be there waiting. With your apples."

"Of course, Your Grace."

After exchanging good-byes and good wishes with the governor, Liza curtsied and left.

For Liza, the week stretched out more slowly than a lazy river.

She kept the apple tucked away in the basket and removed it each morning only to shine it. Perhaps her imagination ran wild, but the apple seemed with each sunrise even more beautiful, more ripe, and more delicious.

Poor Kate. Polish the apple though she might, Ian's finger-prints still sullied the gorgeous scarlet skin. The fruit had lost the brilliance and the value it once possessed. Trying to convince herself that she was only sharing its beauty with those around her,

Kate placed it on the kitchen table. She even accused Liza of selfishness for keeping hers hidden away. But Liza knew in her heart she was doing the right thing. The governor had not given her the apple for others to enjoy, not even for her own delight. He had entrusted it to her care for Claude on that special day when he would set up his fine new household.

Let Kate point her finger all she wanted; Liza would continue on exactly as planned. Mother

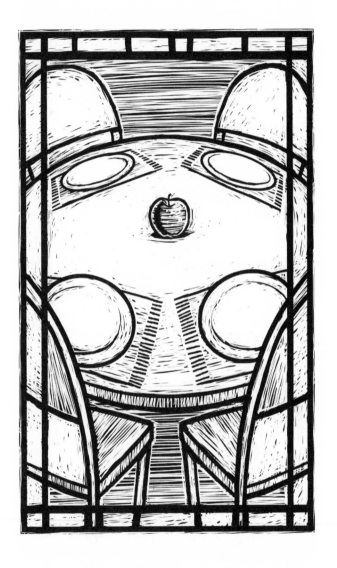

and Father both agreed, but not too loudly lest they hurt Kate's feelings. For although Kate was more beautiful than most, and so a little vain, and careless as well, they loved her and wanted only the best for her.

Soon Ian had spread the news of Kate's beautiful apple far and wide. Islanders knocked on the door begging for a peek. Kate, happily the center of attention, showed off the apple with pride. Ian's fingerprints concerned her at first. But before long, after

hearing all the compliments and flattery-filled pleadings to hold the fruit, Kate relented, letting the onlookers take the apple into their hands.

The son of the admiral of the navy was a handsome fellow named Stuart and was one of the most sought-after young men on the island. When he looked deep into Kate's eyes and asked for a bite, Kate lost all reason. She'd admired Stuart from afar ever since she could remember. Like someone in a trance, she offered

the fruit up to him, and as his hand reached forward, she panicked for a moment, thinking about what would happen next week on the steps of Claude's home. But Stuart caressed her cheek and complimented her on her eyes, hair, and feet. Before Kate could gather her senses, his bite mark marred the precious skin. The sweet meat inside at once began to wither.

And Stuart, having gotten what he wanted, left.

After that, Kate cared little

about the apple. One bite or seven or twelve, what did it matter? Imperfect, unwhole, unlovely, it would never please the governor's son. Not now. Not ever. But perhaps her beauty might win his favor. Men appreciated a comely face and a winning smile more than apples anyway! Yes, she would make sure that Claude had never seen a prettier girl than Kate Carpenter. She sunned her face so that her skin glowed with a coppery cast and her fair

hair shimmered in long golden streams. She flaunted her beauty before her sister.

Poor Liza became more unsure of her attributes with each passing day. But she persisted in her plan, certain that in a few days' time she would hold out her basket and watch Claude lift out the perfect fruit, smile, and say, "Well done!"

A plain girl like her could at least hope for that.

Of course, his eyes might then turn to Kate, and the sight

of her graceful beauty would ensnare him, ushering him into love for her alone. And Liza would stand there, holding out an apple, accepting the position of house-keeper, while Kate was invited to flounce about in fancy dresses, attend endless parties, and order her sister about.

After such thoughts, Liza considered pitching the apple into the bay, but something inside her, all the love and prayers heaped upon her by Mother and Father, bade her to hang on tightly,

respect what she'd been given, hope for the best, and cling to the belief that her sacrifice would deliver its own reward.

The seventh day dawned over the island like a warm Easter morning sun after a windy, rainy night. Liza threw back the bedclothes and jumped to her feet. What lay ahead remained a mystery, but she prepared herself as well as she knew how.

Kate prattled on with excitement at breakfast, more beautiful than Liza had ever seen her. Mother had rolled her shining hair in rags the night before, and curls played about her face like water sprites. Her blue eyes mirrored the splendor of the sky and the sea, and her lips, pinker than geraniums, smiled as though the best day of her life had just begun.

Liza suspected maybe it had, despite the condition of Kate's apple. Her sister's fruit—bitten, brown, and a soppy mess—turned

Liza's stomach. But Kate didn't seem to care at all. Liza wished she might own such confidence.

Nevertheless, Liza bound her dark hair in a scarlet ribbon to match the apple, and slipped into her best gown, simple and pale yellow, and not nearly as pretty as Kate's.

It won't get any better than this, she thought with a sigh.

Hand in hand, the sisters set out toward Claude's new home. Her step light, Kate chattered and waved to all her friends. But

Liza squirmed uncomfortably in the grip of her own nerves. Still, poor Kate. That apple remained the saddest little piece of fruit Liza had ever seen. Even now, Kate held it behind her in a small drawstring bag.

By the time they reached the marble steps of the ornate home, painted a cheerful salmon color, thirty minutes remained until noon.

Liza checked the contents of her basket one last time. Good. Just right. That morning's polish

added the final touch of perfection. "Nervous, Kate?"

"Not really." Kate set her bag on the steps and sat down. "I suppose you think you've got this job sewn up, don't you, with your perfect little apple?"

"I know no such thing. We probably are just two of many invited today. More girls may come striding up any minute now." Liza could hardly believe she was voicing her biggest fear.

"Trust you to think of that, Liza!"

Liza wanted to say, "And there may be *beautiful* girls with perfect apples as well as looks." But why should she bother? *"What will be will be,"* Father always said. *"You try your best, hold your breath, and say a prayer."* Soon enough the day would be done and all events gone the way of a theater play. Hopefully not a tragedy.

But as the sun inched toward its midday summit, no other young women joined them.

Finally the courthouse clock

chimed the noon hour, and the sisters stood to their feet. Liza tucked her basket safely to her side. Kate pinched her cheeks and bit her lips, rousing the lovely pink lying dormant beneath, then reluctantly picked up her bag. Liza attempted no such measures. Like it or not, she could pinch and bite all day and would only look swollen and blotchy, not fresh and breeze-kissed like Kate.

At the final stroke of the clock, a glorious carriage rolled up to the steps. The white horses tossed

their heads, ivory manes jumping about their corded necks. Their silver harness bells jingled and sparkled like diamonds in the sunshine. A footman, liveried in powder blue, jumped down and opened the door.

Out stepped the governor, hale and hearty in his naval uniform. He nodded at the girls. "Good morning, ladies!"

Liza bobbed a curtsy. Kate, did too.

"May I present my son, Claude St. Juste."

First a polished boot emerged through the carriage doorway, then the jeweled hilt of a sword in its scabbard. As the young man unfolded himself from within the carriage, Liza saw a muscled thigh clothed in the dress blues of his uniform, a strong, gloved hand gripping the frame of the opening, then his solid upper body. Finally, his face appeared.

A smile lit Liza's face. Such a pleasant-looking young man. His brown hair, shot through with blond, waved back from his

forehead, and he possessed the clearest, lightest eyes she had ever seen. Ocean waters, and all he'd experienced on his voyages, rested in them. Fine lines, etched by years in the sun, gathered around them and set off the kindness of his gaze.

And his friendly smile. Oh yes! So warm, so generous. Certainly better-looking men inhabited the island. Claude's features were rugged and strong, unlike the refined faces she'd seen in portraits

at the palace. But an aura of confidence and peace painted his features into an intriguing and altogether eye-catching picture.

The governor puffed out his chest with pride. "Girls, my son, Claude St. Juste. Claude, sisters Liza and Kate Carpenter."

Claude clasped Kate's right hand and Liza's left and bowed over them, grinning broadly. "The honor is mine."

Kate covered her mouth, stifling a sweet laugh.

Liza froze, trying her best to

stop staring. "M'lord," was all she could muster.

"Father has told me all about you. In fact, I remember you as little girls." He was looking right at Liza. "You are the elder, are you not?"

"Yes sir."

"And you, Kate. I hear you have a laugh that rings through the streets and brings a smile to all who hear it."

Liza felt a boot of disappointment firmly kick her stomach. It was all over, apple or not. Perhaps

she could persuade Claude St. Juste to hire her as well, in some lower position. Oh, but working under Kate's authority! Doing all the work while Kate received all the credit. She could think of nothing worse.

The governor stepped forward. "Shall we go in?"

They followed him into the grand house.

"Father, it's every bit as magnificent as I've heard."

"I trust you will be quite happy here, Son."

"How could I not?" He looked into the faces of the girls. Kate squealed softly with delight, but Liza felt more ill with every step.

Finally they stood inside the entry hall, papered in bright yellow and adorned with intricate molding and dazzling mirrors. An impressively carved staircase wound upward from both sides of the hall and led to rooms with purposes Liza could only imagine. Music room. Drawing room. Game room. What else? Much to

clean. She knew that. But better cleaning in a mansion than laundering smelly clothes down by the docks. Or marrying some slovenly hooligan. Or, well, the possibilities formed an endless queue. None of them were something in which a girl could revel.

The governor started up the stairs. "Come along. We'll have tea and then admire those apples."

Kate visibly stiffened. But Liza felt an undeniable peace. The basket hung snugly on her arm, held in place against her waist by her

elbow. She well knew her apple's beauty, how she had cared for it, how sweet it would taste if Lord Claude cared so much as to take even the smallest bite. Unable to stop herself, she felt a smile creep onto her face. Truly, she felt sorry for Kate, but not so sorry as to extinguish her own peace of mind. Kate had chosen her path; Liza had as well. It wasn't a pretty fact, but there it sat.

The governor gestured toward a pale blue sofa. "Please be seated, ladies." Claude sat in a chair near

Kate, the governor near Liza. This was not at all surprising to Liza.

The tea arrived at the hands of a manservant, but Liza could not eat the fancy cakes or sandwiches, her stomach flip-flopped so. Kate managed to consume a small plate of food. She delicately lifted each morsel to her pink mouth, all the while smiling sweetly and laughing demurely at the governor's jokes. Liza's hands shook like her granny's, and she almost spilled her tea more than once. Would this interminable

small talk never end? Really, now! All this to find a housekeeper?

Claude set down his cup. "Father, may we proceed? I'm most anxious to move forward."

"Ah yes, Son. Let's begin."

The manservant unobtrusively cleared away their meal, and soon the girls sat on the edges of their seats.

Claude smiled at them both. He reached into his pocket and pulled out...an apple! A beautiful, golden apple. Yellow and ripe. Symmetrical and shining.

His expression welcomed, but his words were serious. "I've been waiting for this day for what seems like years. All during my many journeys I've longed to come to a home of my own and feel cared for and cherished. And I've longed to provide that same care for someone else."

The governor sniffed with pride, folding his hands across his stomach. "Indeed. I made a promise to your father years ago regarding the welfare of you girls."

This definitely sounded to Liza

like more than just a search for housekeeper. And if so, she might just as well pack up and go home. For what young, healthy man would choose a plain girl like her over the stunning, bubbly Kate? What man wouldn't want to see that beautiful face across the table every day or take her fine figure into his arms after a voyage? And imagine the children they'd have!

Claude raised his eyebrows. "And now, ladies, let's begin. Liza, you are quiet and serious,

but a light of peace shines from your eyes. Kate, oh Kate, when you smile the very sunlight seems to catch its breath."

This is the end, then. Liza wanted to cry.

The young man raised a finger. "But surely the proof of who you are rests in how you've cared for the apples I sent to my father." He cocked his head. "So, may I then?"

Kate pulled her bag onto her lap. "Oh sir. I believe this apple was cursed from the beginning. First, Ian got his fingerprints on

it, and polish as I might, they wouldn't come off." Kate continued her explanation, each word deflating her confidence. Liza felt sudden pity at the feebleness of her sister's excuses as they piled one upon the other.

Claude kept smiling. "Surely it can't be as bad as that, Kate. Come now, let's see it."

As Kate drew open the bag, tears filled her eyes. Sobs shaking her shoulders, she pulled out the rotting apple. "I'm sorry. I'm sorry."

Claude's smile vanished. "Oh Kate," he whispered.

"But I can make up for it! I'll serve you well. I promise I'll do anything." She held the apple out to him. "Please take this anyway. Please. And let me serve you."

"But, Kate, if you could not keep this fruit shining and new for only a week, how can I trust you with my heart?"

"But the others... People were so nice, and their interest was so exciting. I was helpless."

"Kate," asked Claude, "why did they have to see the apple in the first place?" He gently pushed her hand away, refusing to touch the apple. "A simple no is all you needed to say. I'm sorry, but you have failed the test. It is a shame, really. You're such a lovely girl, but beauty counts for only so much, doesn't it?"

"You have no heart, sir!" Kate sobbed. She shoved the apple back into her bag and fled from the room.

Tears filled Liza's eyes.

74

Claude knelt down before her. "I'm sorry, Liza. I know you love your sister."

She nodded.

"But the truth of the matter is, the request was not difficult. You see, I have something to give. Something sweet and wonderful, and I only ask for the same in return. God help me, but I've never been willing to take what I'm not willing to give."

"I understand."

"So now, will you show me your apple? May I see if you've taken

your responsibility as seriously as I've taken mine?"

"Of course, m'lord."

Liza set her basket on her lap. As she opened the top, her grief for her sister began to fade, for Kate's actions belonged to Kate alone. Liza had tried to warn her, had offered to help find a safe place. But Kate refused. Liza remembered the time she'd spent polishing the fruit, the way she hid it from all who might see, the way she cared for it like the most fragile of flowers from the most

secret of glades. And she opened the lid with joy, knowing she'd done her best.

"Here it is, m'lord. I've kept it for you." She tilted the basket. "There were moments, when I saw all the attention given to Kate, that I wondered whether guarding the fruit was worth my trouble."

"And I experienced peculiar struggles as well, Liza." Claude held forth his apple. "Equally lovely, yes?"

She laughed, a bubble of joy escaping her throat. Here she

sat facing the governor's son, a strong man in his own right. And she'd prevailed, finding the strength within to protect the treasure that was of far more value than she'd even realized. She felt like laughing, throwing her arms wide, and spinning in a circle.

"By Jove!" said the governor and thumped his son on the back. "I do believe that apple is more beautiful than when I gave it to her, Claude."

"I can believe that." He looked

up from the apple into Liza's face, and his smile was inviting. "I knew it, Liza. I knew it would be you. You do know what's going on, don't you?"

"I believe so, though it seems unbelievable."

Claude glanced at his father. "You see, Father, I told you she was brilliant." And he took her hands in his.

He remained on one knee and asked a question Liza thought she would never hear from a man so daring and noble and brave as

this man before her, a question she sometimes thought she'd never hear at all.

Of course, she said, "Yes!" Wouldn't you?

The governor puffed out his great chest as the sun shone in lemony ribbons on the crowd gathered before the palace balcony. He'd never been more proud of his son and wasn't shy about letting anyone who approached him know it.

Mr. and Mrs. Carpenter, smiles stretching their faces, nearly pinched themselves to make sure it wasn't a dream. And Liza rivaled the sun itself, feeling beautiful for the first time in her life. Even Kate couldn't out-shine her.

Liza's wedding day. Joy filled her from marrow to skin. How worth the wait, the trials, the misunderstandings.

Kate stood beside her sister, happy. Liza said life always gave second chances. And Kate would

grab at her chance with both hands, the first step being pleased for her sister.

Claude held Liza's hand, kind eyes gentling her nervousness as he promised to love her always, acknowledging they would have storms to weather but that he would never leave her side. Liza agreed, promising the same. And the bishop pronounced them married.

Later that afternoon, when they were alone, Liza placed her

ruby apple into Claude's hand. "Take a bite," she whispered.

He placed the golden apple into her waiting palms. "Only if you do the same."

Gazing into each other's eyes, each tasted of the fruit, then closed their eyes at the powerful sweetness that filled their mouths.

The End

Dear Girlfriend

Most likely you've read *Apples of Gold* because your mom, grandmom, aunt, or someone very close thought it might be meaningful to you. I hope it was.

A long time ago I stood in your shoes, unsure about issues of

sexuality and intimacy and a little anxious about what my later
teen years would throw at me. I
grew to maturity in the seven-
ties, a time of sexual freedom
when pretty much the only rule
was that there were no rules.

Now, of course, we know more.
We're more aware of unwanted
pregnancy, abortion, sexually
transmitted diseases, and AIDS.
But the messages thrown at you
on television shows, commer-
cials, and movies only show one
side of the picture, failing to

fess up to the consequences that will affect you for the rest of your life. It's dishonest at worst, irresponsible at best.

Apples of Gold is romanticized. It's a fairy tale. Saving yourself doesn't guarantee you'll find that handsome prince, but it does guarantee you a heavy dose of self-respect. As my daughter has been growing up, we've had many discussions about self-respect and saving yourself—because you know you deserve

more from your initiation into womanhood than sneaking off with someone behind your parents' backs, and because you're far smarter than to fall for the notion that sexual activity will provide any sort of lasting intimacy. You're valuable in ways that might never come to light if you start on the path of physical intimacy before your circumstances warrant it. I've always believed those circumstances must include marriage.

The bottom line, my friend, is if you're not ready to have a baby, you're not ready to have sex.

As I contemplated my future, I thought a lot about the children I would have someday. I never wanted to have to tell them to wait, if I hadn't chosen to myself. I felt like I'd be giving them permission to go out and do likewise if I couldn't do it myself. And so the years went by, and finally I got married, and both my husband and I made it to the altar as virgins. It was definitely worth

the wait for our own sakes. But I have to tell you, the fact that I can now look my children in the eye and counsel them to wait from the perspective not of someone who messed up but of someone who listened to the Spirit and made the right decision, is priceless. And all the credit goes to God who gave me, and will give you, the strength to see it through.

Waiting is so very worth it. Save yourself for marriage not just because it's right but because, in the end, you can look

yourself in the mirror and stand without apology in testimony that you were smart enough to make a wise decision. Ask God to help you persevere.

I'll be praying for you too. I've set up a blog space just for you where you can leave your name: www.lisasamson.typepad.com/apples.

Love,
Lisa

Dear Mom

Or Dear Aunt or Grandmom or whoever cares about the young lady who reads this book.

Apples of Gold is a fairy tale. We know that staying pure doesn't guarantee a prince of a guy or living happily ever after. This little book is merely a tool

to enable discussion between you and the teenage girl you care about. We know that the issue of purity is very complex. The pressures are great not only from peers but also from the overall tenor of societal communication on this issue. People who desire to wait are sometimes seen as judgmental do-gooders who think themselves better than those who are on the path of sexual activity. They are also seen as wet rags, frankly, spoiling all the fun.

Too much is at stake in the life

of a teenager, however, to ignore or put our stamp of approval on behavior that leads to great heart-ache. God wants us to stay pure because God knows this is the path of least pain. We must certainly still love those who have failed to maintain their sexual purity and meet them with grace and encouragement to begin again. God's mercies are new every morning.

If you cannot give the gift of your own personal commit-ment to purity because your past

decisions weren't as wise as they should have been, might I suggest that an apology is in order? When we sin against our bodies and ourselves, we sin against our children too. Purity seems to be a generational blessing, and the commitment to it is something God honors. Encourage your daughter or granddaughter or niece or dear friend to be the first in a line of blessing. Admit your guilt to her, tell her you're sorry, and pledge your own commitment to her. Support her in

every way possible to help her realize her wisdom potential and to become the woman God made her to be, with self-respect intact and grand purpose in front of her. The greatest gift a girl can give herself is her own purity and healthy self-worth.

Nobody benefits from a self-righteous prude. Speak frankly and honestly with your daughter about issues of sexuality. Educate yourself on the temptations and pressures she faces. Life is probably not quite like it was

when you were a girl. Love her enough to understand what she's facing. Your shock won't help keep her pure, but your love and commitment, and a whole lot of time invested, will go far.

Grace to you as you journey on this path together.

Love,
Lisa

Acknowledgments

This story popped into my head almost fully developed, but I'm grateful for those who read or heard the story and encouraged me to move forward into an unknown territory: Terri B. on the van ride in Michigan, Will, Michael, Jennifer, and Chris. I'm especially

grateful for my daughter Ty who loved it right away and didn't mind saying so. Thanks to Don for the initial enthusiasm and to Dudley for carrying the baton on this one. Laura W., thanks for another one.

Thank you to my readers who've been with me all these years. I hope you will accept this as my gift to you for your daughters and granddaughters.